Titles in this series

Railway Series, No. 17

GALLANT OLD ENGINE

by

THE REV. W. AWDRY

with illustrations by
JOHN T. KENNEY

EGMONT

EGMONT

We bring stories to life

First published in Great Britain 1962
This edition first published 2002
by Egmont Books Limited
239 Kensington High Street, London W8 6SA

Thomas the Tank Engine & Friends

A BRITT ALLCROFT COMPANY PRODUCTION

Based on The Railway Series by The Rev W Awdry

© Gullane (Thomas) LLC 2004

5 7 9 10 8 6 4
ISBN 1 4052 0347 1

DEAR FRIENDS,

On the second page of *Four Little Engines* Rheneas was taken away to be mended. He was away for a long time, but has now come home.

All the Little Engines are together at last. They are delighted. Rheneas is their hero. He had saved the Railway. . . .

There is a *real engine* like Rheneas. His name is Dolgoch, and his home is at Towyn in Wales.

Some years ago *he* saved the Talyllyn Railway. We are proud of our gallant old engine.

THE AUTHOR

ACKNOWLEDGMENT

The author gratefully acknowledges the help given by fellow members of the Talyllyn Railway Preservation Society in the preparation of this book.

3

Special Funnel

PETER SAM's funnel had never been quite the same since his accident with the slate trucks. Now, as he puffed up and down the line, the winter wind tugged at it, trying to blow it away.

"My funnel feels wobbly," he complained. "I wish the Thin Controller would hurry up with my new one. He says it will be 'Something Special!'"

"You and your special funnel!" said the other engines, and laughed.

They were all fond of Peter Sam; but he talked so much about his special funnel that it had become quite a joke.

The winter weather worried Mr Hugh. Wind broke branches from trees, while rain turned hillside streams into torrents which threatened to wash the line away.

Mr Hugh and the men patrolled the line every day with Rusty. They removed branches and cleared culverts so that the water could flow away. But one morning they found bad trouble.

A fresh torrent had broken out, and Mr Hugh had to stop all trains. "There's been a 'wash-out' near the tunnel," he said. "The track-bed is swept away."

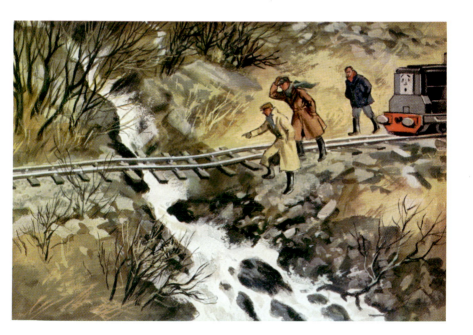

The men worked hard and repaired the damage in a week. While they worked, the weather changed. It became frosty and very cold. They finished just in time for Market Day, and Peter Sam took the morning train very carefully over the mended piece of line.

The tunnel was short, but curved, so they could not see right through it. Suddenly the Driver shouted, "There's something hanging from the roof!" He braked. There was a clanging crash. When Peter Sam and his coaches stopped in the open air, he no longer had his funnel.

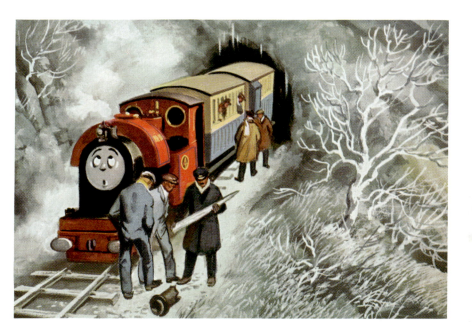

The Guard found the funnel and a thick icicle. "That's what hit you, Peter Sam," he said.

They started again, but the Passengers grumbled at the smoke, so when the Fireman saw an old drain-pipe, they stopped and wired it on.

The engines laughed and laughed when Peter Sam came home. Sir Handel made up a rhyme:

"Peter Sam's said again and again,
  His new funnel will put ours to shame,
  He went into the tunnel,
  And lost his old funnel,
  Now his famous new funnel's a drain!"

They teased Peter Sam dreadfully, but his new funnel arrived quite soon.

"Oh dear!" he said, "someone's squashed it."

The Thin Controller laughed. "It's a Giesl, the most up-to-date funnel there is. Listen! When you puff, you draw air through your fire to make it burn brightly. With your old funnel puffing is hard work. It uses strength you need for pulling trains. Your new funnel has special pipes which help the air come easily. Puffing will be easier, so you will have more strength for your work."

"Yes, Sir," said Peter Sam doubtfully.

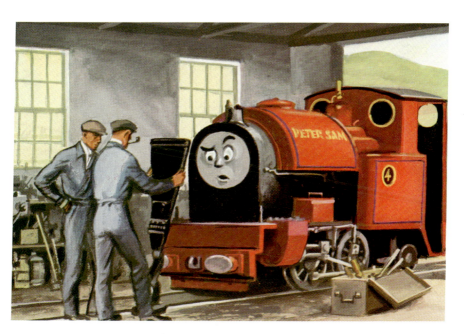

At first Peter Sam's special funnel was a great joke. Sir Handel and Duncan asked him why he had sat on it, and then hooted with laughter. But when Peter Sam started work it was a very different story.

Even Sir Handel was impressed. "I can't understand it," he said. "Peter Sam never seems to work hard. He just says 'Tshe, Tshe, Tshe, Tshe,' and simply strolls away with any train he's given. He makes it look so easy!"

They don't laugh at Peter Sam's funnel now. They wish they had one like it!

Steam-roller

SIR HANDEL kept slipping between the rails, so they gave him new wheels with broad tyres.

The other engines teased him. "Look at his 'steam-roller' wheels," they laughed.

"You shut up!" Sir Handel snorted. "You're jealous. My wheels are special, like Peter Sam's funnel. Now, I'll go faster than any of you."

"You'll never!" The engines were surprised. Sir Handel's trains were usually late.

Skarloey winked. "With your grand new wheels, Sir Handel," he said gravely, "you're just the engine to tackle George."

"Who's George?" Sir Handel asked.

This story is adapted from an incident in Narrow Gauge Album *by Mr P. B. Whitehouse. We gratefully acknowledge his permission to use it.*

While Sir Handel was in the Shed waiting for his new wheels, workmen had come to widen the road which ran for a mile or two beside the railway. They pulled down the wall, and nothing now protected the line.

George was their steam-roller. He chuffered to and fro, making rude remarks when the engines passed. "Railways are no good," he would say. "Pull 'em up. Turn 'em into roads."

Skarloey had often heard that talk before, and he warned the others to take no notice; but he hoped that, when the two boastful engines met, he and the others would have some fun!

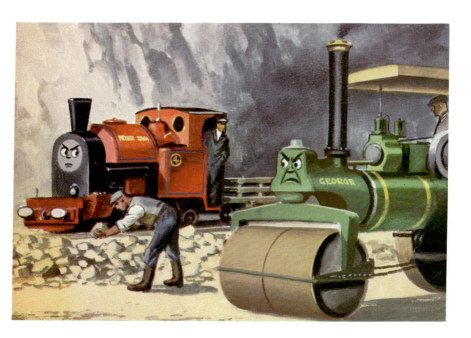

"Don't worry any more," said Sir Handel importantly when they told him about George. "Leave him to me. I'll soon send him packing."

Next morning George was standing near the Halt by the Level Crossing. "Huh!" he said. "You're Sir Handel, I suppose."

"And you, I suppose, are George. Yes, I've heard of you."

"And I've heard of you. You swank around with steam-roller wheels, pretending you're as good as me."

"Actually," said Sir Handel sweetly, "I'm better. Goodbye." He puffed away.

George chuffered, fuming.

One afternoon Sir Handel had to bring a special load down after the last train had gone. When he reached the road, he saw George trundling home.

"Peep-pip-peep!"

George took no notice. He trundled along close to the track. There was barely room to pass.

"Peeeep-pip-pip-peeeeep!" Sir Handel slowed and crept cautiously alongside. "Get out of my way, you great clumsy road-hog," he hissed.

"I don't move for imitation steam-rollers," retorted George with spirit.

They lumbered along side by side, exchanging insults.

No one could ever explain what happened next. George's Driver says he signalled for Sir Handel to stop. Sir Handel's Driver says he signalled to George.

There was a crash. The brake-van tilted sideways, and the Guard scrambled out to find George's front roller nuzzling his footboard. The two drivers were hotly arguing whose fault it was.

A policeman strolled up in time to stop the argument turning to fisticuffs, and when Sir Handel's Fireman came back with Rusty and Mr Hugh, they all set to work clearing up the mess.

Neither engine had been going fast enough to cause much damage. So Sir Handel was able to bring his train on when George had backed himself away.

Next day, the workmen put up a fence between road and railway and then went away, taking George with them. This was because they had finished their work; but Sir Handel thought *he* had made George go away.

He was more conceited than ever, and talked everlastingly about steam-rollers.

"Oh dear!" whispered Skarloey one evening. "He's worse than ever. I'm sorry my plan was no good."

"Never mind," said Rusty. "We'll think of something else."

But they had no need to do that, for some boys came and asked Mr Hugh if they could look at the engines. Almost at once one called out, "Look! Here's Sir Handel. He raced a steam-roller last week. The Roller nearly beat him too. It was most exciting."

Sir Handel never mentions steam-rollers now!

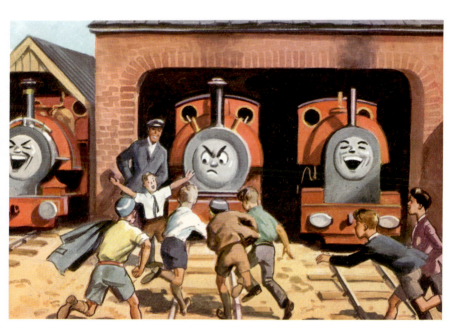

Passengers and Polish

NANCY is a Guard's daughter. She was working on Skarloey with some polish and a rag.

"Wake up lazy-bones!" she said severely. "Your brass is filthy. Aren't you ashamed?"

"No," said Skarloey sleepily. "You're just an old fusspot. Go away!"

She tickled his nose. "Rheneas comes home tomorrow. Don't you want to look nice?"

Skarloey woke suddenly. "What! Tomorrow!"

"Yes, Daddy told me. I'm going now."

"Nancy, stop! Do I look really nice? Please polish me again. There's a good kind girl."

"Now who's an old fusspot?" laughed Nancy.

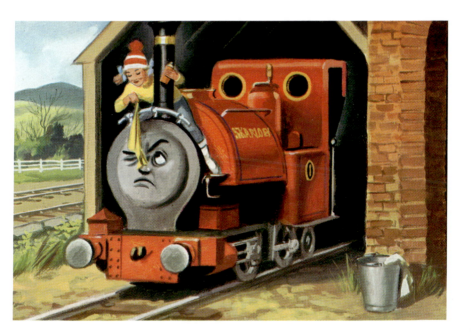

She gave him another rub, then climbed down.

"Aren't you going to polish me?" asked Duncan.

"Sorry, not today. I'm helping the Refreshment Lady this afternoon. We must get the ices and things ready for the Passengers on Skarloey's two o'clock train. Never mind, Duncan, I'll give you a good polish tomorrow."

But Duncan did mind. "It isn't fair!" he complained. "Peter Sam gets a special funnel, Sir Handel special wheels, Passengers get ices, and I'm never even polished."

This, of course, wasn't true; but Duncan liked having a grievance. He began to sulk.

That afternoon a message came from the Station by the Waterfall. "One of Skarloey's coaches has come off the rails. Please send some workmen to put it right."

Duncan was "in steam", so he had to go.

"All this extra work," he grumbled, "it wears an engine out!"

"Rubbish," said his Driver. "Come on!"

The derailed coach was in the middle of his train, so Skarloey had gone on to the Top Station with the front coaches. Duncan left the workmen, and brought the Passengers in the rear coaches home. He sulked all the way.

He arrived back just in time for his own four o'clock train. "I get no rest! I get no rest!" he complained.

He was sulky and short of steam, so his Driver waited a few minutes in the hope of raising more; but Duncan wouldn't try.

"We can't keep the Passengers waiting any longer," his Driver said at last.

"You always think about Passengers," muttered Duncan crossly, "and never about *me*. I'm never even polished. I'm overworked, and I won't stand it."

He grumbled away, brooding over his "wrongs".

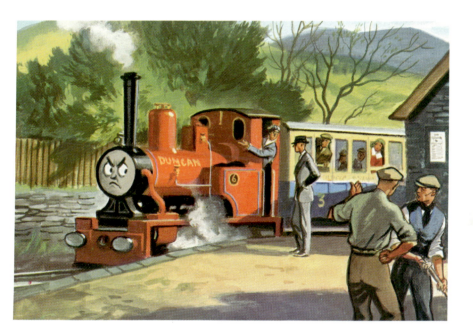

Duncan made "heavy weather" of the journey, but at last they reached the Viaduct. This is long, high and narrow. No one can walk on it when a train is there.

"Come on, Duncan!" said his Driver. "One more effort, and you'll have a rest and a drink in the Station."

"Keep your old Station!" said Duncan rudely. "I'm staying here!"

He did too! He stopped his train right on the Viaduct, and nothing his Driver or Fireman could do would make him move another yard.

Skarloey came from the Top Station to haul Duncan and his train to the platform. The Passengers were very cross. They burst out of the train, and told the Drivers, the Firemen, and the Guard what a Bad Railway it was.

Skarloey had to pull the train to the Top Station, too. Duncan wouldn't even try.

The Thin Controller was waiting at the Shed for Duncan that evening. He spoke to him severely. But Duncan still stayed sulky. He muttered to himself, "No polish, no Passengers," in an obstinate sort of voice.

Gallant Old Engine

"I'm ashamed of you, Duncan," said Skarloey. "You should think of your Passengers."

"Passengers are just nuisances. They're always complaining."

Skarloey was shocked. "That's no way to talk," he said. "Passengers are our coal and water. No Passengers means no trains. No trains means no Railway. Then we'd be on the scrap-heap, my engine, and don't you forget it. Thank goodness Rheneas is coming home. Perhaps he'll teach you sense before it's too late."

"What has Rheneas to do with it?"

"Rheneas saved our Railway," said Skarloey.

This story is adapted from an incident in Railway Adventure *by Mr L. T. C. Rolt. We gratefully acknowledge his permission to use it.*

"Please tell us about it," begged Peter Sam.

"The year before you came," said the old engine, "things were very bad. We were on our last wheels. Mr Hugh was Driver and Fireman, while the Thin Controller was Guard. He did everything else too, *and* helped Mr Hugh mend us in the Shed.

" 'We expect two fresh engines next year,' they told us, 'but we *must* keep the trains going *now*; if we don't, our Railway will close.' "

"How awful!" said Peter Sam in sympathy.

"I tried hard, though I couldn't do much, but Rheneas understood. 'It's my turn now,' he said. 'You've done more than your share of hard work.' "

He was often short of steam, but he always tried to struggle to a Station, and rest there. "That," said Skarloey earnestly, "is *most* important with Passengers."

"Pshaw!" exclaimed Duncan.

"Passengers," Skarloey continued, "don't mind stopping at Stations. They can get out and walk about. That's what Stations are for. But they get very cross if we stop at wrong places like Viaducts. Then they say we're a Bad Railway, and never come back.

"I remember Rheneas stopping in a wrong place once," said Skarloey. "He couldn't help it. But he made up for it afterwards.

"That afternoon he had damp rails and a full train. There were Passengers even in Beatrice, the Guard's van. His wheels slipped dreadfully on the steep bit after the first Station, but they gripped at last. 'The worst's over,' he thought. 'Now we're away.'

" 'Come along, come along,' he sang to the coaches. 'Come al—— Oooooh! I've got Cramp!' he groaned. He stopped, unable to move, on the loneliest part of the line.

"The Thin Controller and Mr Hugh examined him carefully. The Passengers watched and waited. Rheneas eyed them anxiously. They looked cross.

"At last the Thin Controller stood up. 'Your valve gear on one side had jammed,' he said. 'We've unfastened the rods and tied them up. Now Rheneas,' he went on, 'we need to reach the next Station. Can you pull us there on one cylinder?'

" 'I'll try, Sir, but the next Station isn't the right Station. Will the Passengers be cross?'

" 'Don't worry,' smiled the Thin Controller. 'They know we can't reach the Top Station today.'

"The Thin Controller sanded the rails, Passengers from Beatrice pushed behind; Mr Hugh gently eased out the regulator. The train jerked and began to move.

" 'I'll ...do .... it! I'll ...do .... it!'

"Everyone cheered, but Rheneas heard nothing. 'The Thin Controller's relying on me. If I fail, the Railway will close. It mustn't! It mustn't! I'll get there or burst.'

"Everything blurred. He was too tired to move another yard; but he did! And another ... and another ... and another ... till, 'I've got there at last,' he sighed with relief.

" 'It's proud of you I am indeed,' said Mr Hugh.

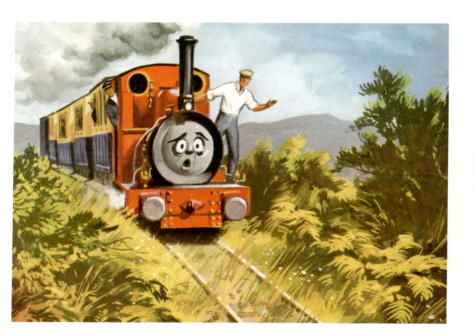

"All Rheneas remembered about the journey down was having to go on going on. At the Big Station the Passengers thanked him. 'We expected a long walk,' they said, 'but you brought us home. We'll come again, and bring our friends.'

" 'You're a gallant little engine,' said the Thin Controller. 'When you're rested, we'll mend you ready for tomorrow.' "

"Was Rheneas always 'ready for tomorrow'?"

"Always," smiled Skarloey. "Whatever happened, Rheneas always pulled his trains."

It was Duncan who broke the silence. "Thank you for telling us about Rheneas," he said. "I was wrong. Passengers *are* important after all."

All the Little Engines were at the Wharf on the day that Rheneas came home. Some of the Fat Controller's Engines were there too.

Edward pushed Rheneas' truck to the siding, and Skarloey pulled him neatly to his own rails. This was the signal for a chorus of whistles from engines large and small. You never heard such a noise in all your life!

The Owner, Rheneas, and other Important People made speeches, the Band played and everyone was very happy.

But Rheneas was happiest of all in his own place that night, next to his friend Skarloey. "This helps a little engine to feel," he said, "that, at last, he has really come home."

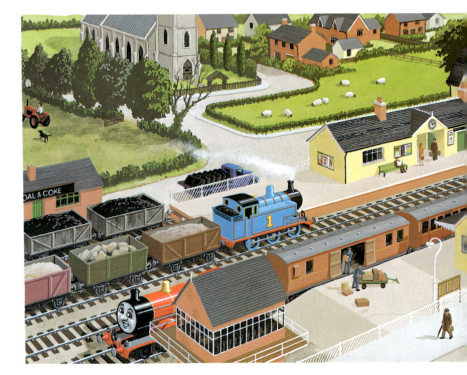